A Valentine for You

Wendy Watson

Clarion Books · New York

SOURCES

Baring-Gould, William S. and Ceil Baring-Gould, eds. *The Annotated Mother Goose*. New York: Bramhall House, 1962.

Botkin, Benjamin A., ed. *A Treasury of New England Folklore*. New York: Crown Publishers, 1947.

Delamar, Gloria T., ed. *Children's Counting-Out Rhymes, Fingerplays, Jump Rope and Bounce-Ball Chants and Other Rhythms: A Comprehensive English-Language Reference*. Jefferson, North Carolina: McFarland & Co., 1983.

Emirch, Duncan, ed. *American Folk Poetry: An Anthology*. Boston: Little, Brown & Co., 1974.

Newell, William W., ed. *Games and Songs of American Children*. New York: Dover Publications, 1963.

Opie, Iona and Peter Opie. *The Lore and Language of Schoolchildren*. London: Oxford at the Clarendon Press, 1959.

———, eds. *The Oxford Dictionary of Nursery Rhymes*. Oxford: Oxford University Press, 1951.

———, eds. *The Oxford Nursery Rhyme Book*. Oxford: Oxford University Press, 1955.

Calligraphy on jacket and title page by Paul Shaw.
Clarion Books
a Houghton Mifflin Company imprint
215 Park Avenue South, New York, NY 10003
Illustrations copyright © 1991 by Wendy Watson
All rights reserved.
For information about permission to reproduce
selections from this book, write to Permissions,
Houghton Mifflin Company, 2 Park Street, Boston, MA 02108.
Printed in the USA

Library of Congress Cataloging-in-Publication Data
Watson, Wendy.
A valentine for you / Wendy Watson.
p.   cm.
Summary: Love songs and rhymes are accompanied by illustrations of
a family's celebration of Valentine's Day.
ISBN 0-395-53625-1
1. Children's poetry.   2. Nursery rhymes.   [1. Love — Poetry.
2. Nursery rhymes.   3. Valentine's Day.]   I. Title.
PZ8.3.W345Val   1991
782.42164′0268 — dc20   90-2699
                                                                                        CIP
                                                                                        AC

HOR 10 9 8 7 6 5 4 3 2 1

FOR CECIL

Roses are red, violets are blue,
Sugar is sweet,
And so are
you.

Good Mother Valentine,
God bless the baker!
Who'll be the giver?
I'll be the taker.
The roads are very dirty,
My boots are very clean,
And I've got a pocket
To put a cookie in.

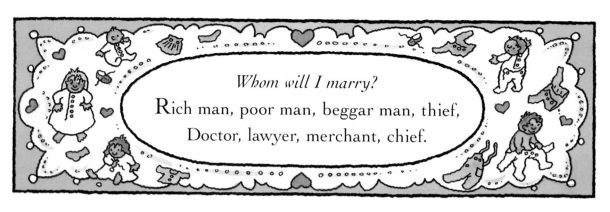

Whom will I marry?
Rich man, poor man, beggar man, thief,
Doctor, lawyer, merchant, chief.

What will I wear?
Silk, satin, calico, rags.

How will I get there?
Coach, wagon, wheelbarrow, chaise.

Where will we live?
Big house, little house, pigsty, barn.

If you find a hairpin,
Stick it in your shoe.
The next boy you talk with
Is sure to marry you.

He loves me.
He don't!
He'll have me.
He won't!
He would if he could,
But he can't,
So he don't.

A pretty little girl in a round-eared cap
I met in the street the other day;
She gave me such a thump
That my heart it went bump—
I thought I should have fainted away!

As I went walking down the street,
Down the street, down the street,
A pretty girl I chanced to meet,
Heigh ho, heigh ho, heigh ho!

Rig-a-jig-jig and away we go,
Away we go, away we go,
Rig-a-jig-jig and away we go,
Heigh ho, heigh ho, heigh ho!

As I went walking down the street,
Down the street, down the street,
A handsome boy I chanced to meet,
Heigh ho, heigh ho, heigh ho!

Rig-a-jig-jig and away we go,
Away we go, away we go,
Rig-a-jig-jig and away we go,
Heigh ho, heigh ho, heigh ho!

The rose is red, the violet's blue,
The honey's sweet, and so are you.
Thou art my love, and I am thine;
I drew thee to my Valentine.
The lot was cast and then I drew,
And fortune said it should be you.

Lilies are white, diddle, diddle,
Rosemary's green,
When you are king, diddle, diddle,
I shall be queen.
Roses are red, diddle, diddle,
Lavender's blue,
If you'll have me, diddle, diddle,
I will have you.

Joan Smith   Emily Jones   Susie White

Molly Cook

Jane Brown

Linda Green

Annie Jackson

Barbara Adams

Sarah Brown is her name,
Single is her station.
Happy is the little man
Who makes the alteration.

John and Mary sitting in a tree,
K-I-S-S-I-N-G!
First comes love, then comes marriage,
Then comes Baby in a baby carriage.

Alice   Jack   Tom   Paul   George
      Lizzie   Barbara   Linda
                          Kate

Ella, Ella, dressed in yellow,
Went downstairs to meet her fellow.
How many kisses did he give?
One, two, three, four…

        Trina   Sarah   Holly
  Jerry   Lewis
Joan   Cliff   Roger

Oh, dear doctor, can you tell
What will make poor Annie well?
She is sick and like to die,
And that will make poor Peter cry.

Oh, Charlie's sweet and Charlie's neat,
And Charlie he's a dandy,
Charlie he's the very lad
That feeds the girls on candy.

You ought to see my blue-eyed Sally,
She lives right here in this old valley,
Number on the gate and number on the door,
The next house over by the grocery store.

A tisket, a tasket,
A green and yellow basket,
I wrote a letter to my love
And on the way I dropped it.

I dropped it, I dropped it,
And on the way I dropped it,
I wrote a letter to my love
And on the way I dropped it.

Mailman, mailman, don't delay,
Do the rhumba all the way.

S.W.A.K.

Mollie, my sister, and I fell out,
And what do you think it was all about?
She loves coffee and I love tea,
And that was the reason we couldn't agree.

Billy gave me apples,
Billy gave me pears,
Billy gave me fifty cents
And kissed me on the stairs.

I gave him back his apples,
I gave him back his pears,
I gave him back his fifty cents
And kicked him down the stairs.

Oh, dear, what can the matter be?
Dear, dear, what can the matter be?
Oh, dear, what can the matter be?
Johnny's so long at the fair!

He promised to bring me a basket of posies,
A garland of lilies, a garland of roses,
He promised to bring me a bunch of blue ribbons
To tie up my bonny brown hair.

And it's oh, dear, what can the matter be?
Dear, dear, what can the matter be?
Oh, dear, what can the matter be?
Johnny's so long at the fair!

Oh where, oh where has my little dog gone?
Oh where, oh where can he be?
With his ears cut short and his tail cut long,
Oh where, oh where can he be?

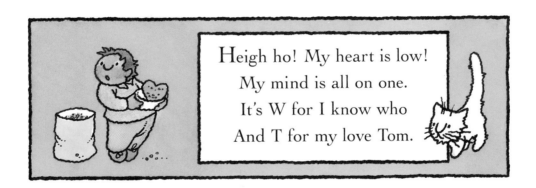

Heigh ho! My heart is low!
My mind is all on one.
It's W for I know who
And T for my love Tom.

Let's go to the wood, says this pig.

What to do there? says that pig.

To look for my mother, says this pig.

What to do with her? says that pig.

Kiss her to death, says this pig.

Pa, Pa, build me a boat,
Pa, Pa, build me a boat,
Pa, Pa, build me a boat
To sail across the ocean.

Come, my love, set by me,
Come, my love, set by me,
Come, my love, set by me,
And sail across the ocean.

Pa, Pa, build me a boat,
Pa, Pa, build me a boat,
Pa, Pa, build me a boat
To sail across the ocean.

My pen is black,
My ink is pale,
My love for you
Shall never fail.

My love is like a cabbage
Divided into two.
The leaves I give to others
But the heart I give to you.

Down in the valley, the valley so low,
Hang your head over, hear the wind blow.
Hear the wind blow, dear, hear the wind blow,
Hang your head over, hear the wind blow.

Write me a letter containing three lines,
Answer my question, will you be mine?
Will you be mine, dear, will you be mine?
Answer my question, will you be mine?

Roses love sunshine, violets love dew,
Angels in heaven know I love you.
Know I love you, dear, know I love you,
Angels in heaven know I love you.

If you love me, love me true,
Send me a ribbon, and let it be blue.
If you hate me, let it be seen,
Send me a ribbon, a ribbon of green.

Follow my Bangalorey man,
Follow my Bangalorey man,
I'll do all that ever I can
To follow my Bangalorey man.
We'll borrow a horse and steal a gig
And round the world we'll do a jig,
And I'll do all that ever I can
To follow my Bangalorey man.

Wash and wipe together,
Live in peace forever.

I hate to wash the dishes,
I hate to scrub the floor.
I'd rather kiss my sweetheart
Behind the kitchen door.